Dedication:

For Shauna & Christina
Real Princesses in training

A Real Princess

Colleen Connors

AuthorHouse™
1663 Liberty Drive, Suite 200
Bloomington, IN 47403
www.authorhouse.com
Phone: 1-800-839-8640

First published by AuthorHouse   5/5/2009

ISBN: 978-1-4389-6884-1 (sc)

Printed in the United States of America
Bloomington, Indiana

This book is printed on acid-free paper.

authorHOUSE®

Foreword

This story is for all girls who know that
deep down inside, they are a princess.

And who grow up to find out
that all along...they were right.

There once was a little girl
who loved to play dress up.

She would pretend to be a lot of different characters,
but her favorite person to dress up as was a princess.

She would ask her mother, "Mommy, am I a princess?" and her mother would answer, "No, you are just my daughter."

She would tell her brothers, "My real parents are a queen and king."

Her brothers would laugh and say, "You only wish you were a princess." But deep down inside the girl longed to hear that she truly was a princess.

She would spend hours trying on different fabrics, arranging them around herself in elaborate, fancy, ways to make herself look as princess-like as she could imagine.

She would wear her mother's jewelry in creative ways; combining earrings and necklaces, bangles and rings, to make herself feel golden, rich, and exotic, like a princess from a far away land.

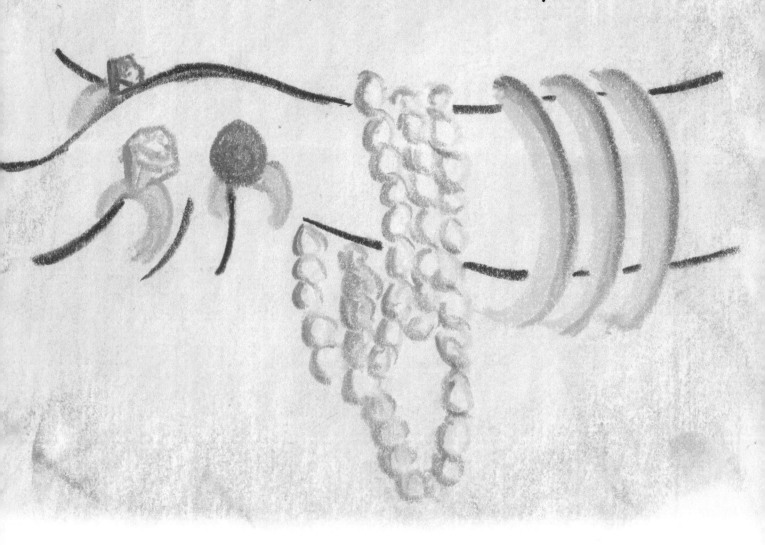

The years passed, and the little girl grew into a young lady and forgot about wanting to be a princess.

She went to work and dressed up only for special occasions. Gone were the days of spending hours day-dreaming with fabrics and jewels.

But something inside of her
still longed to be more.

One day, she met a king. Even though she was now grown up, the king told her that He wanted to adopt her as His daughter.

He told her that he had always wanted to adopt
her, and that He had been waiting her whole
life for her to hear His voice and listen.

The king told her He knew how she had longed to be a princess. He told her that all she had to do to be a princess NOW, was to accept His invitation to become His adopted daughter.

Also, she had to forget all her past mistakes and forgive the people who had hurt her. Lastly, she had to live like a princess.

LIVE LIKE A PRINCESS!
Can you imagine what that meant to her?!

Most people imagine royal balls and festivals,
beautiful clothes and jewels, hired servants and palaces.

Others think of travel and fame and doing what ever you want, whenever you want.

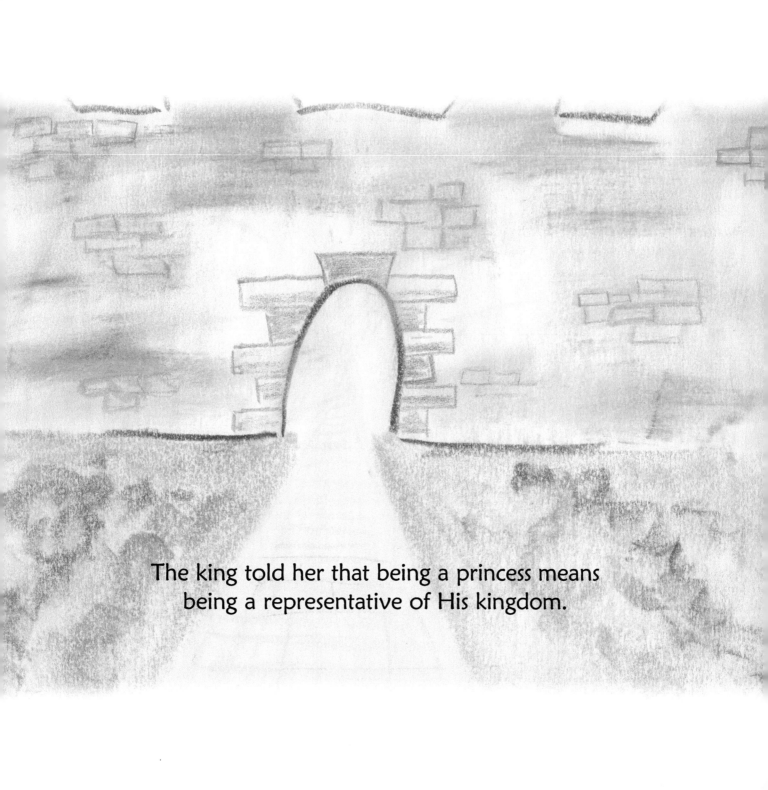

The king told her that being a princess means
being a representative of His kingdom.

To be a good representative was to do things she had not thought about much, before.

Things like thinking of other people's needs, serving others before her self, and speaking only positive of others.

The king told her to prepare for the future by using her money, time, and talent, to help others. He taught the woman to be more compassionate and caring in the relationships with the people in her life.

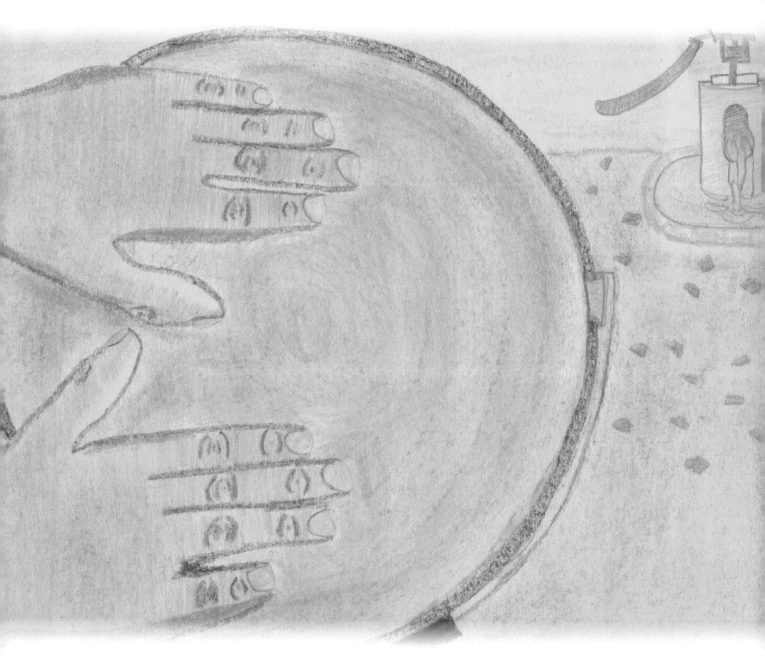

She learned to reach out to others in need. She learned that people have differing needs. She found that having strength and dignity was better than having a fancy dress or jewels.

She no longer fantasized over
luxurious clothes and palatial estates.

She learned that charm is deceptive and beauty does not
last, but a woman who is full of respect for others and loves
others no matter what, is what being a princess is all about.

The little girl, who felt as though she should be a princess, grew into a woman who became a princess! She accepted the king's invitation for adoption. She accepted what it means to be a princess.

Because she did, she was transformed
in the presence of the King.

Over the years she
grew in all the kingdom
ways of selflessness.

She grew in joy,
kindness, gentleness,
faithfulness,
patience,
goodness,
self-control,
and peace.
Love now ruled her
heart and mind.

She is now a
princess
forever more.

She shares her story with you, so that little girls
everywhere can know how to be a real princess, too!

Printed in the United States
146666LV00001B